ONE WINTER NIGHT

Jennifer Lloyd

Illustrations by
Lynn Ray

One winter night
Under moonlight
Out of their nest,
So full of zest,
Climbed ten grey mice
Onto the ice.

H

"oot," went owl
On the prowl.

Hurry, hurry,
Scurry, scurry,
Went one grey mouse
Back to his house.
Nine little mice
Pranced down the ice.

ut leapt squirrel,
Tail in a curl.

Hurry, hurry,
Scurry, scurry,
Went one grey mouse
Back to his house.
Eight little mice
Pranced down the ice.

"F

lap, flap," went bat,
Swooping by rat.

Hurry, hurry,
Scurry, scurry,
Back to his house
Went one grey mouse.
Seven little mice
Pranced down the ice.

long hopped hare
Out of his lair.

Hurry, hurry,
Scurry, scurry,
Went one grey mouse
Back to his house.
Six little mice
Pranced down the ice.

Skunk crawled by,
Tail on the fly.

Hurry, hurry,
Scurry, scurry,
Went one grey mouse
Back to his house.
Five little mice
Pranced down the ice.

ut for a stroll,
Slowly roamed mole.

Hurry, hurry,
Scurry, scurry,
Back to his house
Went one grey mouse.
Four little mice
Pranced down the ice.

A long slipped fox
On icy rocks.

Hurry, hurry,
Scurry, scurry,
Went one grey mouse
Back to his house.
Three little mice
Pranced down the ice.

ext strutted deer,
A doe right near.

Hurry, hurry,
Scurry, scurry,
Went one grey mouse
Back to his house.
Two little mice
Pranced down the ice.

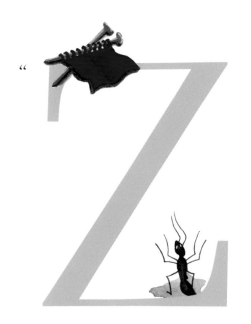

"zz, Zzz" snored bear
Without a care.

Hurry, hurry,
Scurry, scurry,
Went one grey mouse
Back to his house.

One brave, grey mouse,
Far from his house,
Far from the mice,
Pranced down the ice.

Slinking, creeping,
Creeping, slinking,
Across the snow,

Came a shadow
With some whiskers,
Long thin whiskers
And pointy ears,
Black pointy ears.

Halt went brave mouse,
Far from his house.

"Purr, purr," went Cat,
Furry and fat,
"Squeak! Squeak!"
went mouse,
Far from his house.

Hurry went mouse,
Scurry went mouse,

Past purring cat,
Furry and fat,
Past snoring bear,
Without a care,
Past strutting deer,
A doe right near,
Past slipping fox,
On icy rocks,

P

ast roaming mole
Out for a stroll,
Past skunk crawling by,
Tail on the fly,
Past hopping hare,
Out of his lair,

Past flapping bat,
Swooping by rat,
Past leaping squirrel,
Tail in a curl,
Past hooting owl,
On the prowl.

afe in his house,
Sneaked the small mouse,
One winter night,
Under moonlight.

The End

First published in 2006 by Simply Read Books
www.simplyreadbooks.com

Book design by
Robin Mitchell for hundreds & thousands

Library and Archives Canada Cataloging
in Publication

Lloyd, Jennifer
 One winter night / Jennifer Lloyd : illustrated by Lynn Ray.

ISBN-10: 1-894965-48-5   ISBN-13: 978-1-894965-48-4

 I. Ray, Lynn II. Title.

PS8623.L69054 2006   jC813'.6   C2006-901364-0

Printed in Singapore

10 9 8 7 6 5 4 3 2 1

We gratefully acknowledge the support of the Canada Council
for the Arts for our publishing program.

To Pierre, Patrick and Emily — J.L.

To my family Alan, Lisa, Nicole, Jeff & Jon, Dianne, Frank,
Tiffany & Darren and my parents, Sylvia & Paul for inspiration,
love and support and to Christianne Hayward and
Christine Leplante for direction and encouragement. — L.R.